I0689070

Homecoming

Angélique Jamail

also by Angélique Jamail

Animal Affinities series:
Finis.

Poetry:
The Sharp Edges of Water

ADVANCE PRAISE FOR *Homecoming*

"A fantastical looking glass on the modern world and the timeless hurdles of growing up."
— Seth Skorkowsky, author of *Ashes of Onyx* and *Dämoren*

"With *Finis.* and now *Homecoming*, Jamail has created a rich, nuanced world in which the line between human and animal is blurred. The lines demarcating which is which are often used by people to put others in their place. And with a sharp irony, the monstrosity of those with their Animal Affinities is most shown in how they choose to treat their Plain friends and family — that is, by the very human choices they make, not the animal instincts that infuse their characters. These are beautifully written, poignant, and often funny stories, which fans of both the speculative and the literary will enjoy immersing themselves in."
— David Jón Fuller, contributing author to
Parallel Prairies, On Spec, Tesseracts

Homecoming

Book 2 of the Animal Affinities Series

Angélique Jamail

Odeon Press

Published by Odeon Press.
www.odeonpress.com

ISBN 978-1-7328629-4-4

Edited by Jayne Pillemer.
Cover and interior graphic design by Lauren Volness.
Book formatting by Jesse Gordon.

for my own Taita (1922-2001):
I'm so grateful to have her recipes
and for the hours I spent learning to cook with her

for Aaron:
because every book I write is also for you

for everyone else who needs to read this:
I see you
You matter
You are necessary

Table of Contents

Author's Note..17

1...19

2...37

3...51

4...57

5...69

6...77

7...95

8...101

Acknowledgements...115

Book Group Discussion Questions.................117

Respect..119

Ways to Support Authors................................127

About the Author...129

Author's Note

While most of the names in this book are going to be very easy to pronounce, there are two I want to give a quick guide for because they are Arabic names and might not seem to necessarily follow the usual English conventions for pronunciation.

Raqia should sound like "RAH-kee-uh." It is widely considered a Muslim name with Urdu origins, but there are certainly women with this name who don't identify with either Islam or Urdu.

Taita should sound like "TIE-Tuh." It is a term in Lebanese Arabic (and perhaps also in other dialects) which means grandmother, but which also has affectionate connotations. Unlike in English, where a second instance of a consonant sound might be somewhat muted, both "t" sounds are specifically pronounced. In my family, multiple grandmothers are all called Taita, but with their first names given to distinguish them; for example, I called my grandmother Taita Rose and my great-grandmothers Taita

Mary and Taita Liz. This word is also frequently spelled "teta" or "tita," but I have chosen the spelling "taita" to help distinguish it from other languages where "teta" and "tita" refer to different familial relationships.

I also want to make one note about the cover art for this book. The design was created by Lauren Volness, who also executed the beautiful cover art for *Finis*. For *Homecoming*, she began with a base image by artist Archan Nair entitled "Only One." I remain in awe of both these artists' incredible talents, and I am forever grateful for how unbelievably patient and easy to work with Lauren is.

I

WALKING HOME from school on Thursday, Raqia tells her best friend Anabelle, "This week has been stupid long."

Anabelle nods. "As long as a swan's stretched neck." She knots her blonde ponytail into a bun and shifts her backpack to the other side. "Lord Jesus, I'm so ready for the weekend."

It's late September in Houston, and the trees are still as green as ever, the sun hot enough to make the girls sweat through their t-shirts. Raqia lifts the thick black braid hanging down over her shoulder and piles it on top of her head to catch the furtive breeze.

"This weather would be so much easier if we were birds," Anabelle continues. She lifts her arms toward the sky and makes graceful, determined flaps as if she might actually surprise herself by taking flight. "I wonder if we could create our own air currents." She looks at Raqia with a hopeful seriousness. "Do you think the feathers would be noticeable for long? Are they insulating or cooling?"

Raqia shrugs. "Taita doesn't have hers anymore," she says, referring to her grandmother. "I don't think they last longer than pinfeathers." Then she grins. "And I'm pretty sure she's never actually flown—outside of an airplane."

"Oh, *ha*." But Anabelle isn't really annoyed because she can't completely hide her smile. "Do you think you'll have the same Affinity she has?"

Raqia shrugs again. Animal Affinities don't really run in families very often, and Raqia hasn't shown any sign of hers at all yet, so there's no telling how she'll turn out.

Then Anabelle sighs and kicks a small crumble of cement into the yard they're passing. "I'm really tired of waiting," she mumbles.

"Yeah." There's no point in saying much else about it. They're both already in eleventh grade, and neither has shown any hints of their selves at all. Raqia knows—they both know—that it isn't unusual to get most of the way through high school before evincing definitive signs. So Raqia tries not to worry about it yet.

"It just feels like everyone else at school has found their Affinity already," Anabelle continues, shuffling lightly through purple wisteria blooms that have fallen onto the sidewalk.

Raqia nods. She longs for the ability to feel grown-up and powerful, confident like the girls who prance around campus, all fluttering feathers in their long hair and strong footfalls in their gait. They know they belong, and where.

Nothing can touch them. And that doesn't make the waiting any easier. She and Anabelle are both weary of being written off as Plain Ones.

"It's been a long week," Raqia says again.

The summer is one thing. They don't spend a lot of time around the other kids from school when it isn't in session, so their Plainness—their *presumed* Plainness, Raqia reminds herself—isn't often tossed in their faces. But this August, even more of their peers came back all figured out, their animal natures evident and sometimes on full bragging display. Ready to be considered full people by the adult world. So many of them, it surprised her a little.

As they turn the corner at the entrance into their neighborhood, someone calls Raqia's name from a driveway just behind them. A few guys from school are lounging next to a car parked there, and one of them, Ramón from her French class, stalks up to her. He has a striking red coxcomb. Normally he keeps it sandy brown like the rest of his hair, but he's gone full scarlet in honor of the game tomorrow night. He stands quietly in front of her. Raqia and Anabelle look at each other in confusion, but before either of them can speak, Ramón crows loudly in Raqia's face, causing both girls to jump. The other guys near the car laugh.

"Looks like you're growing a wattle," Raqia mutters, pointing dismissively at the uneven beard under his chin, also dyed red for the occasion.

Ramón then volleys a word at her she doesn't know, but his inflection and sour expression tell her it isn't meant to be flattering. He says it amid a string of advanced French that includes *Liban,* the name people use to refer to when Lebanon was under colonial rule. She knows enough about history to feel both insulted and a little afraid of Ramón's attitude. A couple of the other guys snicker and one gives a low whistle. Anabelle doesn't speak French at all and looks around uncomfortably.

Ramón lifts his angry eyebrows at Raqia in challenge. *"Et alors. T'as quelque chose à me dire?"*

She translates in her head as quickly as she can. *So then. You have something to say to me?* She wants to tell him off, but she doesn't speak French—or, frankly, Arabic—well enough to do it in either language with real confidence, and in English, her comeback might be parroted back at her by his friends for weeks. Still, she tries hard to remember how Taita had once told an obnoxious telemarketer who wouldn't stop calling their house to piss off in Arabic.

"Oh, look." Anabelle snorts into the awkward moment of silence. "The French kid can speak French. So what? If you really wanted to challenge yourself you'd learn Mandarin. Or whale song."

One of the guys standing by the car laughs at that, too. Ramón takes a step forward toward Anabelle. A woman comes out of the house and calls to someone in the driveway.

"Let's just go," Raqia mutters, pulling Anabelle by the arm and pushing past Ramón, annoyed that she couldn't think of anything better to say. She glances back.

He walks over toward the car in the driveway. One of his friends has painted red tiger stripes across his bulky arms, and another has spiked his hair into horns; they high-five and whoop like the zoo exhibit they are. Tomorrow night is homecoming, and the mania surrounding the football team is enough to make Raqia feel nauseated. She and Anabelle keep walking away, and though they look back over their shoulders now and then, until they've passed the next block, Ramón and his friends haven't followed them.

So yeah, Raqia is ready for the weekend, but she's maybe even more ready for next week, when all of the primate frenzy about this game will be over.

She and Anabelle finally reach Raqia's house. A sign hangs from the streetlamp in the front yard, decrying the loss of a neighbor's platypus. The frantic text offers a hefty reward and warns in large black marker: "Wolves suspected. Proceed with caution." They look at the sign and at each other, and Anabelle glances at her own house across the street, then looks down at her shoes, waiting for an invitation.

"Want to come in and see Taita?" Raqia asks, just like pretty much every day.

"Wouldn't miss it," Anabelle says with a cheery smile.

She likes being specifically invited over. Something about southern manners, she said once; Raqia just rolls with it. It's easier than forgetting to ask and then hurting Anabelle's tender feelings over something that doesn't matter.

When they come through the front door, they find Taita watching a special news bulletin, her face pinched and a half-rolled grapeleaf wilting on the wax paper in front of her. The television is turned up too loud and set at an odd angle, so she can hear and see it from the kitchen table. She jumps at the sound of the door closing.

"Taita, is everything okay?" Raqia asks. She and Anabelle drop their backpacks behind the couch and dutifully walk across the room to greet her.

"Oh, yes, habibti, I'm fine," she insists, wiping the corner of one golden-brown eye. She gives them each a quick kiss hello and turns her attention back to the food in front of her, her sharp fingernails slicing through the larger leaves to make each one the correct size.

"What's going on?" Anabelle asks, gesturing to the television. A shaky cell phone video shows some aggressive looking guys scattering outside a store front somewhere. It's hard to tell what's happening: the phone zigzags around as its holder obviously runs from the fray, and the noise of people shouting and cars stopping short, of someone trying to direct people around the area, muddies everything. The news anchor's voice-over trying to make sense of things only adds to the confusion.

"Wolf packs again," Taita answers, pushing her large round glasses up onto her beaky nose.

"Did they say who?" Anabelle asks, biting her lip. "Is it here in Houston?"

The anxious clench of Raqia's stomach comes on quickly. At summer's end, the packs started prowling around, making trouble in Dallas and San Antonio. It started as pranks, a few busted-up mailboxes and the air let out of a police car's tires. A bunch of young twenty-some-things acting out on their wolfish natures. But things esca-lated when some guy home from college was beaten up—badly—for being Plain, even though it is possible for one's Animal Affinity to emerge in adulthood. Theoretically.

"I heard a few weeks ago, some packs have turned up in Galveston and Beaumont," Taita says, resignation sitting heavily in her throat. "It's like Beirut all over again." The infamous Beiruti wolf packs, their violence, drove Taita to emigrate, although no one else in the family had been willing to leave. Even Raqia's widowed father stayed be-hind, citing his important position at the Université Saint-Joseph de Beyrouth. He made no objection to his mother's taking her only grandchild with her. Raqia was three. "And now they've found wolves in Magnolia," Taita con-tinues, waving a moist hand at the television.

"That's still a ways off," Anabelle says, but she looks un-comfortable. Magnolia is only an hour and a half away. "And I'm praying every day that it stays a long ways off."

But Houston is the biggest city in this region, so it's just a matter of time before a wolf pack forms here.

Taita sighs and murmurs softly in Arabic. Raqia knows what that means. Taita left behind family, friends, and homeland to protect her granddaughter from the wolf menace. Once they emigrated, she focused on speaking English to integrate into their new home. Raqia's own use of their native tongue has lapsed considerably in the last several years, but she catches in her grandmother's tone the flavor of a lament, a phrase that suggests they might as well have stayed in Lebanon.

The news anchor describes a litany of offenses the pack in Magnolia has perpetrated over the last week. It seems they've graduated from smashing car windshields to robbery. The candid video is back, now that the phone's owner has apparently moved far enough away from the action to get a decent shot. Raqia watches the pack fleeing the scene. They have on jeans and black concert t-shirts and wear their hair long and shaggy; they howl and holler to each other as if in glee against a soundtrack of sirens and burglar alarms. The butcher whose shop they've blown over stands in his doorway shouting and waving a cleaver. His apron, stained with the smears of his trade, reads "Joe's Halal Meats."

Raqia's insides churn as she remembers the stories Taita told her about Beirut. She has always taken comfort in the idea that the bad wolves are confined to another part of the world, even while feeling guilty that she doesn't mind if they are in her homeland, as long as they aren't in her home-now. She might feel worse if her father doesn't insist, every time Taita calls him, that he is safe. Most wolves aren't the university type.

Suddenly the footage on the television zooms awkwardly on what must be the alpha, from the way he's directing the others. His face flashes across the screen too fast to be identifiable, and the camera focuses on the wads of money he's stuffing into his jeans pockets. He shouts some guttural command at the others then bounds away just before the first police car arrives. Soon an officer comes up to the bystander filming and shuts down his phone. The news report cuts back to the anchor, who introduces an Affinities Behavior Psychologist from Texas A&M University.

"Being a wolf is different from having other Animal Affinities," this Dr. Crystalle Delacourt explains. She has golden skin and a wild mane of hair that frames her noble face. "Whereas most people enjoy animal traits that enhance their appearance or senses or even talents, over time more wolves are evolving to become more lupine than human, and the path to that transformation—especially lately, as we've seen—can sometimes go savage."

Anabelle fidgets and begins playing with her hair, chewing on her lip. Raqia recognizes the signs of her anxiety.

"The historical record shows it was not always this

way," Dr. Delacourt continues. "The change began around one hundred fifty years ago but was so gradual at first, the best accounts we have of it are only anecdotal. Perhaps one in a thousand violated the bounds of polite society. The greatest shift we've seen, this trend toward violence, has become more pronounced only in the last generation or so. Preliminarily, we suspect that increased social divisiveness, the growing polarization in politics and other cultural wedges, may have something to do with it."

Raqia doesn't need a psychologist to tell her that people are becoming angrier these days, that the world is growing more hostile.

Dr. Delacourt's voice again: "The causes for this are still being studied—which makes a good segue into a new research program I'm heading. We're looking for volunteers, people with wolf Affinities—"

Anabelle turns the television off. "We don't need her commentary," she mumbles. Taita looks at her with compassion. "I'm just tired of hearing about wolves, that's all."

"You are tired of worrying about them," Taita observes.

Anabelle sighs. "I'm tired of worrying about one of them."

Raqia knows her friend has been watching the news report for one reason: to see whether her brother's face will turn up. It doesn't. Eddie, Anabelle's older brother and only sibling, is the kind of wolf who defies the stereotype: he isn't a Big Bad.

"It's frustrating," Anabelle says. "I can't understand

why sometimes I'm worried sick about him, and sometimes I just wish he'd go away and live his own life somewhere else far apart from mine."

Sometimes Eddie and Anabelle get along and sometimes they don't, just like any siblings Raqia has ever observed. She doesn't think this is a big deal, but as she lacks any brothers or sisters of her own, Anabelle is rarely inclined to listen to what Raqia has to say on the subject. It occurs to her that Anabelle could be worried their fighting might increase the odds Eddie might turn Bad.

"This is all just sensational anyway," Raqia says, gesturing to the television. "Plenty of wolves don't turn into criminals. But the normal ones with normal lives don't make it onto the news."

Taita clucks under her breath and turns back to her grapeleaves. "I don't know, habibti, I don't know." She sniffs. "These wolves today are not like the wolves I knew when I was your age. Back then, a wolf and a lamb could still be friends."

A couple of years ago, when news broke of the first pack on American shores, Taita lectured Eddie soundly about pack wickedness, but he swore nine ways to Sunday that he wasn't involved in any of that. Taita has known Eddie for years, ever since elementary school when he and Anabelle started spending most of their free time at Raqia's house. Otherwise, Taita might have banned him from her home when his Affinity showed up.

Raqia puts an arm around Anabelle. "*Some* of the wolves have turned bad, but some definitely have *not*." She waves dismissively at the television. "Nothing about those guys means anything for anyone else."

Her friend hugs her back. "It's like I keep telling Eddie," she says. "Pray away the prey."

Raqia gives her a half-hearted nod at the platitude; she doesn't think prayer is going to stop a wolf's predatory instinct, but there's no shaking Anabelle's faith. She herself would feel better if science could figure out why the wolves are changing. She heard some Affinity Behavioralists talking about it on a radio program lately, about how the most brutal lupine instincts seem to be following other negative social trends: gang violence, crime rates, even corporate and political corruption are all spiking in places where the wolf Affinity shows the most concentration. But no one has yet offered any reliable conclusions why, at least not that Raqia and Anabelle have heard about.

They join Taita in the kitchen.

"Can we help?" Raqia asks.

Taita swivels her head around to smile at them. "If you like," she says. After washing up, the girls sit at the table and pull sheets of wax paper and a short stack of grapeleaves in front of them. Taita long ago taught them how to roll an inch or two of raw lamb and rice into a tender leaf, to wrap it tightly so it won't unravel in the boiling pot. "How was school?" she asks.

Raqia shrugs. She doesn't want to tell her grandmother about the rando bully who was a disparaging ass to her and Anabelle in the lunchroom. Anabelle came back from gym class a little dewy, and when her moist hands left prints on the table, he slug-shamed her and loudly commented that he was going to start carrying a box of salt with him. "It was fine."

"Homecoming is tomorrow," Anabelle says, blushing as a smile replaces her worry over the news report.

"Ah, I'd forgotten!" Taita clucks. "Homecoming—I never did understand. How are the football players coming home? Whose home are they going to?" Her grin is subtle. "It never made sense to me."

Raqia and Anabelle both groan at the old joke. "You know that's not what it's about, Taita!" Anabelle says, her hands pausing mid-roll. "It's just a name. The alumni are coming home to watch the game."

Raqia didn't know that was the idea behind the word, though she has always liked the sound of it. "Home-coming" calls to mind permanence and predictability. Something a person can depend on being there when they need it.

"Are you girls going to the game?"

"No," Raqia says. Eddie was starting quarterback in high school, and Anabelle was required by their parents—their dad, mostly—to show up when he was playing. She insisted Raqia go, too, to keep her company, even though neither of them like football: it's just a bunch of loudly grunting boys crashing into each other, proving how rhino they are, no matter their Affinities. Raqia hopes they can spend their Friday nights doing more fun things now that Eddie has graduated. She has visions of movie nights and pedicures and taking silly magazine quizzes instead of getting a sore bottom from sitting on cold metal bleachers for several hours.

"We're definitely going to the dance Saturday night," Anabelle says, smiling, her mood improving by the minute. "Taylor asked me to go out to dinner at Franco's and to the dance with him." Her crush, the one taking her to homecoming, the one guy Anabelle has ever liked who doesn't seem to mind that her Affinity hasn't come out yet.

"Ah," Taita says. "Franco's is very nice."

Raqia gives her grandmother a sly grin. "She hasn't been this excited since Eddie left for college." Raqia will go out to eat with Taita and meet up with Anabelle and Taylor at the dance later, since she doesn't have a date herself.

When they finish rolling the grapeleaves, Taita carries them to the enormous boiling pot on the stove and drops them carefully in, then covers them with water and lemon slices.

"Do you want to stay for dinner?" she asks Anabelle, who shakes her head.

"Thanks, but Eddie came home today, and I'm supposed to be there." In high school he was an All-American, and this is Texas, where football is practically a religion. No chance Eddie won't come back for his alma mater's homecoming game.

Raqia smirks. "Hail the conquering hero."

Anabelle looks at her while she washes her hands. "I was hoping you'd come over, too."

"Are your parents also going to be home?" Taita asks, her eyes narrowing into keen circles.

Anabelle snorts. "Oh, they wouldn't miss their favorite boy in the world."

Raqia wonders sometimes whether Anabelle worries so much because their parents seem to worry so little. Eddie can do no wrong in his father's eyes, after he proved himself such an alpha on the football field.

Anabelle looks back at Raqia. "Do you mind?"

And suddenly Raqia wants to. It will make her feel better to see Eddie—fun-loving, friendly, not malicious in any way. The news bulletin has unsettled her. She wants to be reminded that not all wolves are criminals. "I don't mind," Raqia says then looks at Taita. "Can I go over to Anabelle's house and buffer her from her scary older brother?"

"Rocky!" Anabelle swats her with a dish towel. "Don't tease!" Raqia giggles and snaps her own towel back.

Taita laughs, a throaty sound that shakes her shoulders and feathered, brown-and-gray hair, but it's strained. "Of course," she says, then points to the grapeleaves she has already boiled. "And take him some of those. He can't get them homemade up at school."

Anabelle hugs her. "Thank you, Taita."

"But you must get your homework done." The girls both nod. "How much do you have tonight?"

"Only biology and history." Raqia's two favorite subjects. "I've done everything else."

"I don't have much, either," Anabelle says. "Some math, and the same bio homework Rocky has. We can work on it together."

Taita nods. "That's fine. But come back home by ten, habibti," she warns Raqia. "It's still a school night. And you never know who's prowling around in the dark."

2

RAQIA KNOWS the first thing Anabelle will do when they get to the Fosters' house is try to find her cat. It's the same every time. Anabelle bursts through the front door and drops her backpack immediately; Raqia moves it out of the way so she won't trip and puts hers next to it.

"Chuy!" Anabelle calls in a singsongy lilt. "Where are you?" She checks the chairs in the dining room to see if the cat is hiding under the table. "Meow?"

Raqia stifles a laugh. Anabelle thinks saying meow is like speaking cat and has started doing it ever since Jessika in their math class bragged that her Aunt Lois' cat can understand her when she speaks. Anabelle's efforts haven't produced any results yet with Chuy, though.

"There you are!" Anabelle squeals when she sees the cat lounging halfway up the staircase and runs to scoop it up in a hug. The tabby submits to her affections but doesn't reciprocate. Raqia watches her friend coo at the thing, its tortoise stripes undulating as it wiggles in her grasp.

Soon Eddie saunters through the front door, dark brown hair tousled and wearing an old Def Leppard t-shirt that looks a little too small for him. He's flanked by four other boys from school Raqia doesn't know well. They're seniors who worship Eddie and his full-blown wolf nature even more than his status as a college freshman, although most of them have less wolf in them than a toy teacup poodle. One or two of them are real dogs, Anabelle sometimes says to make Raqia laugh, but both of them know these guys are confident where they will land. As soon as the cat hears Eddie's rumbly voice, it hisses and scrambles away from Anabelle's grip and trips up the stairs as fast as its short legs can move.

Anabelle groans. "Eddie! Why are you always scaring my cat?"

"Hi to you, too, sis," he shoots back, then he bares a smile at Raqia. "Hey, Rocky." He tugs on the side braid she always wears. "Always nice to see you."

"Hey." She points to the kitchen. "Taita sent over some grapeleaves. They're in the fridge."

"Awesome! Tell her thanks." He heads off in that direction, his fanboys following. "You guys won't believe how good this food is."

One of them, with unkempt black hair and bright blue eyes, hangs back. He puts a boot on the bottom step and leans close to Anabelle. "I'll bet kittens taste good, too," he says with a leering grin.

"You leave my cat alone. It's bad enough you're even in my house," Anabelle hisses. Her long blonde hair seems even paler in contrast to her angry red face.

"Watch it, puppyface," Raqia says and pushes his shoulder back. She doesn't know his real name but knows he has a goading disposition Anabelle doesn't like.

He snorts a laugh and saunters off after Eddie and the other guys.

"I don't trust them," Anabelle says through clenched teeth. "Not any of them. Who knows what they'll do once they aren't worried about getting suspended from school anymore?"

"Puppyface sucks," Raqia agrees, "but Eddie's not so bad."

Anabelle scrunches her nose in response. Having them all in her house must put her on edge more than usual.

Then all the guys walk back through the hallway and toward the front door. "I'll be back in a few," Eddie says, his baritone barely audible over their boisterous voices. He stuffs two grapeleaves in his mouth at once on his way out.

Puppyface looks back over his shoulder and blows Raqia a kiss. She rolls her eyes.

Anabelle mutters, "I just *know* one of these days he's going to come home for the weekend and wolf out, and I'm going to walk into my room and find Chuy's bloody guts all over my bedroom curtains!"

Raqia tries not to laugh at the melodrama. "*Wolf out?* What does that even mean?"

"You remember that camping trip he went on, don't

you?"

Eddie found his Animal Affinity really early, in seventh grade. It was a novelty when he gained the ability to grow a full beard over the span of a weekend in middle school.

But on one of his boy scout camping trips, he caught a rabbit and then went a little frenzied when he was supposed to be learning to clean it and dress it for cooking. He tore the thing in half and took a bite out of its raw flank, and for a while some people gave him a pretty wide berth.

"That was six years ago! And your cat is not a wild rabbit, and Eddie has had pretty incredible self-control ever since." Enough even to pacify Taita.

Anabelle shifts her weight and sniffs, a sure sign she doesn't have a rebuttal. "Still," she says.

"Maybe if you talked to Eddie about it, you would feel better."

"I don't want to." Anabelle is closing off; Raqia can see it in the hard set of her jaw. Stubborn. "It won't do any good, anyway. He never listens to me."

"I don't think that's true."

Anabelle glares. "Whose side are you on?"

"No one's—there are no *sides* here."

Anabelle sniffs again. "I'll think about it."

But Raqia isn't sure how much she believes her.

Chuy ventures back down the stairs, now that things are quiet again, and Anabelle coaxes him into her lap with a catnip mouse she keeps in her pocket. Raqia knows she keeps it there in part so people at school will think she needs it for herself on stressful days.

Anabelle found her ancient cat perched on the rim of a dumpster, his tail in the air and his nose buried in a bag of day-old pastries. She begged her mother to let her bring him home. They took him to a vet, who found the animal to be of mature but indeterminate age despite a youthful attitude. That was twelve years ago. Then three years ago, Anabelle decreed the cat might be immortal and renamed him in honor of her favorite person ever, Her Lord and Savior Jesus Christ. His nickname is Chuy, since that seems somehow less sacrilegious.

Eddie calls him The Immortal God-Cat of Westbriar Drive. And when he really wants to upset his sister, he calls him Lunch. Eddie likes to upset his sister a lot, and conflict-averse Raqia has often, over the years, stepped in to smooth things over between them.

He walks back in, alone this time. Before he can speak, Anabelle says, "Your friends are a problem. They shouldn't be coming over here."

"They're fine," Eddie dismisses her. "It's not like you're going to see them much anyway."

"True, you hardly even live here anymore." Anabelle is putting on her priss, and Raqia makes ready to intervene. "It's probably best if your thugs just stay away, since this is still *my* house, and I don't want them here."

"Come on, Anabelle." Raqia's hackles rise at the unfair

name-calling. It hits too close. "They haven't done any-thing to you. Saying they're thugs is a bit much."

"This is my house just as much as it's yours," Eddie says, focused entirely on his sister. The fine brown hairs on his arms stand up. "Technically, it's Mom and Dad's."

Anabelle tightens her grip on Chuy, who mews in protest and tries to squirm away. "You leave my cat alone."

"What? I didn't touch your cat!" His eyes darken. "But maybe one of these days I *will*." He stalks back through the hall and off to the kitchen.

"I just wish he would go back to school," Anabelle seethes. "Everything is easier without him."

Easier, Raqia knows, because she doesn't have to bal-ance her worry for his safety with how much he irritates her. "You know he wouldn't really do anything—he's only trying to annoy you. Why give him the satisfaction?"

Anabelle doesn't have an answer for that and just sits there, huddled into her furious self with Chuy, grinding her teeth.

Raqia has never been able to decide what might be worse, having an Affinity that people are afraid of, that marks her as a threat and even more obvious pariah—or having none at all. Every time she or Anabelle has felt doomed to Plainness, Taita has reminded them, one more time, that there isn't a timetable for this. That it isn't un-usual to get most of the way through adolescence before one's Affinity makes its debut. But their parents all showed their Affinities early, and Eddie's being The Wolf from a young age makes Anabelle even more impatient.

Raqia can't forget the desperate vow Anabelle made them swear in ninth grade that they'd remain best friends forever, just so if they ended up Plain they wouldn't end up alone, too. At first Raqia thought the oath over the top, but when her social life failed to blossom in high school—

Eddie bangs around in the kitchen, still sounding annoyed. He and his sister were close when they were little. And now? Well, he's moving on into the world. People like him, people respect him. He's popular and really always has been. And he has done things the people around him consider worthwhile, and now he's playing football for a college that wanted him on their team so badly they gave him a four-year full ride.

Raqia has yet to demonstrate any extraordinary talent at anything. She wants success in her life, not just for herself, but also to show Taita the sacrifices she made to bring Raqia to the U.S. have been worth it. She has often wondered whether she could make her grandmother proud and get her father's attention by going into an academic field of research, making some important breakthrough or solving some big problem. But she will need to distinguish herself in some way to locate that path, and so far, there isn't much distinctive about her other than the place she's from. And even that—when she doesn't even speak the language—isn't something she feels she can claim with a lot of confidence. Raqia is fascinated by zoa-psychology and wants to study behavioralism in college, but she doesn't imagine any reputable Affinities Studies program will take her if she's Plain.

Not having an Affinity is just one more way Raqia doesn't measure up.

The thought of never reaching her full potential is a scary thing, and it's something she and Anabelle share. Raqia thinks that fear might be what has made Anabelle so religious, praying the rosary and even novenas, even though her evangelical pastor disapproves of such things. Every once in a while someone stays Plain into adulthood, and they've all heard stories of Plain Ones having it rough; sometimes they can't find good jobs or get mortgages. Raqia is afraid of being lonely and alone, looked down upon for not having an Affinity, no matter what else is inside of her. She has often wondered whether Anabelle's weird devotion to Chuy is an attempt to cultivate an animal nature.

Eddie walks back in with a half-eaten loaf of pita bread from the package Taita sent over. A slip of butter and a light dusting of crumbs smear the edge of his mouth. Raqia smells the warm snack and finds herself hungry. He stands in front of Anabelle, who is still stewing on the stairs with her cat.

"Let go of that thing," he says to her, the heat of *his* anger, at least, dissipated. Now he's just the exasperated older brother again. "It doesn't like being held like that." He takes another bite.

"Let him go, why? So you can *play* with him?"

"No," Eddie says, his mouth full. "It clearly doesn't like you." He sighs through his nose and swallows the bread. "Anabelle, you're going to figure out who you are. I have no worries that you won't."

Her eyes water and she relaxes her grip. The cat stops struggling and darts up the stairs. "Do you really believe that?"

"Of course." He smiles at her. "I'm not worried about either of you." He transfers his grin to Raqia. "I can't wait to see how you both turn out."

"That makes three of us," Raqia says, glad the tension between Anabelle and Eddie is evaporating. It's exhausting.

He looks at his sister again, more seriously. "But that cat isn't going to save you."

Anabelle's face closes up again. "We'll just have to see," she says primly. "You don't know everything."

Eddie shrugs. "Suit yourself." He trudges toward the living room and plops onto the sofa and turns on the television. Within just a moment, live coverage breaks in of another pack attack, this time in nearby Baytown, and he swears under his breath and switches the television off again right away. He leans forward, rakes his fingers through his dark hair, rests his elbows on his knees and his chin on his hand.

Anabelle's phone rings from the side pocket of her back-pack, a bouncy dance tune, and she jumps up to retrieve it before the voice mail catches. She smiles, her mood suddenly bright. "It's Taylor," she says. But their conversation, the part Raqia can hear, doesn't sound cheerful. Anabelle hangs up. "I can't believe it. He canceled." She plops back onto the stairs. "He found out Eddie's back and doesn't want to come over."

"Why would he do that?" Raqia sits down next to her.

"This is so stupid." Anabelle shakes her head. "He said maybe he'd see me at the dance." She leans onto Raqia's shoulder and starts crying, the scent of her frustration, the rapid pendulum swing of her emotions, suddenly pungent and alarming.

Raqia pats her hair. "I'm sorry." Her sympathy feels sharp and anxious.

Eddie walks in. "What's wrong with her?"

"She lost her dinner date for the homecoming dance."

Eddie shrugs. "No problem."

"I think it's a problem for Anabelle," Raqia says. "Look at her."

He smiles, and his eyes flicker, two dark stars that suddenly look to Raqia like the whole universe. "Y'all can come with us."

"Why are *you* going to the dance?" Anabelle snarks into Raqia's shoulder. "Aren't you a little *grown-up* for that?"

His glance lights on Raqia for such a short second she

isn't sure she's seen it right. "The guys want me to. What else am I going to do on Saturday night? Everyone will be *there*." He reaches out and pats his sister's arm. "Come on, sis, it'll be fun. Like old times."

Anabelle looks up, her face a puff of pink blotches. "Old times is not what I had in mind." Raqia thinks about how happy Anabelle was when Eddie left for college. She thought her life was going to start fresh. And Taylor seemed like part of that.

"Raqia, convince her." He looks so earnest. "Please." How can his eyes be so dark and so bright at the same time? "Come out with us."

Even though his fanboys irritate her, she hears herself say, "Going to the dance with them won't be that bad." Eddie's look then could consume her. Raqia cocks her head. She can't have missed him while he was off at college, can she? "That's really nice of you."

He grins at her. "All right then."

Anabelle, however, groans. "That's just perfect," she says. "Can't freaking wait."

3

IT TOOK only a few minutes for Raqia and Anabelle to become best friends. Or more to the point, for Anabelle to save Raqia from what she imagined to be the loneliest childhood in Texas. They met in the middle of third grade, when Raqia and Taita stopped living lease to lease and bought a house on the same street where the Fosters lived. The day was chilly, and Raqia took her skateboard out to the driveway to get free of the stuffy house and out from underfoot of Taita and the movers. She was still learning the bumps and cracks of the pavement and hit the narrow wooden divider between two expanses of concrete at a precarious angle. Trying to regain her balance, she accidentally tumbled her skateboard over a mound of bubble wrap that had fallen off the back of the moving truck. The popping sound brought Anabelle and Eddie running out of their garage to see whether someone was setting off fireworks, but it was only Raqia, awkwardly sitting on the concrete, lamenting a skinned elbow and scratched-up shin.

"Are you okay?" Anabelle asked, crouching down to inspect the injuries. Her blonde French braids were so long they almost touched the driveway.

"Yeah, I think so," Raqia said but she winced when she tried to straighten her arm.

"That looks like it hurts," Eddie said. "Do you want us to get your mom?"

Raqia looked down, pretending to be absorbed in her scrapes, but finally shook her head. She didn't have a mom, not anymore, and she didn't remember the one she'd had when she was a baby anyway.

"How about your dad?" Anabelle asked, as if that were the easiest thing in the world to do.

Raqia hadn't seen her father in years. "My grandmother is home," she finally said. "I'll be okay."

"You live with your grandmother?" Anabelle asked, her eyes pinched in confusion.

And why wouldn't she be confused? Raqia had been in Texas long enough to know that most people didn't.

Eddie cleared his throat at his sister with a slight edge in his eyes, and Anabelle looked away. To Raqia he said, "I wish I could live with my grandmother. She's an amazing cook and plays the best card games."

Raqia smiled at him. "Mine too. Canasta is her favorite, but I keep forgetting the rules, so mostly we play Rummy and Go Fish."

He smiled back and gestured toward the house. "Want us to get her?"

But Taita was already busy enough today that she'd squawked at Raqia when she sent her out to play, so she didn't want to bother her. "No, I'll be all right." She stood, but slowly, her left hip twinging from the fall.

"You're bleeding," Anabelle pointed out as she also stood. "Come to our house. We have a first aid kit."

"I don't know…" Raqia hadn't seen which house they'd come from, and she didn't think Taita would like it if she wandered off.

"We live just there," Anabelle said, pointing across the street. "It'll be quick." Her friendly smile made Raqia feel better, so she nodded and let them help her over to their house. They took her inside and helped her bandage up her scrapes, then when they found out she was transferring to their school, Anabelle practically squealed with enthusiasm. "We're going to be such good friends!" she said, and Raqia found herself optimistic at the prospect.

That Monday, Anabelle introduced Raqia around so she wouldn't be lonely at school, and soon the girls became close. Eddie rounded out their trio, although he and Anabelle bickered like crazy as they got older.

Raqia shepherded Anabelle through every math class from sixth grade on, and Anabelle was always the first to comfort Raqia any time a bully at school made fun of her exotic lunches or her prominent nose. They forged a shared history of favorite songs and movies, of Saturday mornings at the museum's dino exhibit and Sunday afternoons swimming with the ducks and riding the carousel at the park. Even as Raqia and Anabelle diverged in their electives and extra-curriculars in high school, they remained best friends. As the ranks of the still-Plain students dwindled each school year, and the collective attitude of everyone else implied those unfortunate peons were pariahs—even to each other—Raqia and Anabelle clung together.

Now in eleventh grade, when so many of their classmates have found their Affinities and formed corresponding bonds that are deeper than just being in classes or on sports teams together, Raqia understands the value of having one good friend.

4

THE DAY of the homecoming dance Raqia goes over to Anabelle's house early so they can get ready together. They have similar dresses: vintage pin-up style frocks with halter-sweetheart necklines and full skirts that stop just above the knees. Anabelle's is cotton candy pink, while Raqia's is turquoise with a small pattern of dark red flowers. Taita generously called the dresses "flirtatious and cute," but her shallow smile made it clear she thought they showed off too much shoulder, collarbone, and leg. Raqia likes that her dress isn't too green for her olive skin and complements her black hair.

Before the game last night Anabelle made a grudging peace with her brother and his unbridled enthusiasm that they would be going with him and his friends to dinner and the dance, but she spent some time hassling him about it first. "Who goes to a high school dance when they're in college?" she asked. The quiet way he responded, without getting angry at her, made the girls wonder if he's really having as fun a time in college as he lets on to the fanboys.

Anabelle admitted to Raqia that it was better than

staying home all night moping, and Eddie has been really nice to them all yesterday and today, even making a point of telling them how much he liked the grapeleaves when he found out they helped make them. But Anabelle's conflicted emotional state resurfaces as she smoothes out the white ruffle around the hemline of her dress.

"I don't know," she says. "I hate being Plain, but it's better than being a wolf. Don't you think so?"

Raqia detects the sour tang of desperation in her voice and pretends to agree. A particularly vile attack on a liquor store late that morning hijacked everyone's news feeds and set off emergency alerts in a ten-mile radius of the store. A lone wolf—already in custody—was the culprit, but still. Anabelle's and Raqia's phones went off like air raid sirens, and Taita called the Fosters' house herself to make sure Eddie was "at home where he was supposed to be." Raqia was already at their house when Mrs. Foster called Eddie downstairs to answer the phone; he lumbered into the kitchen replete with messy bedhead and slouchy pajama pants. He patiently assured Taita that he hadn't even gone outside yet today, but Raqia could tell from his side of the conversation he was getting a thorough lecture on the dangers of wolves who make poor choices with their lives. Waking up to all of this made him grumbly as he cooked himself an omelet.

And now the wretchedness of wolves has been Anabelle's compulsive topic of conversation all afternoon.

Raqia has stopped her from biting her manicure right off, but only barely.

"Look," she finally says, buckling her dressy heels on, "it's not that I don't agree, being a wolf isn't a great thing. But seriously." Raqia stands right in front of her friend and makes her look her in the eyes. "He is your *brother*." She wants to add, *Don't you know what I would give to have a brother? Or a sister? Or anyone besides a grandmother and a father halfway across the world?* "He's not a bad person. He's not a bad wolf. I don't care what the scientist of the day is saying on the hourly news reports. They don't all turn. They just don't."

Anabelle's eyes screw up and she pushes out an exasperated sigh. "I guess we have to believe that, don't we? I sure hope other people do." She shakes her head. "People who know Eddie know he's all right. But what about the ones who don't? The news is so awful lately." She fiddles with a trio of lip glosses on her vanity table. "I just don't want anything bad to happen to him."

"Neither do I."

Anabelle is quiet a moment, then says, "I argue with him too much, I know." She looks up then as if searching for help. "He just sets me off. I don't know how not to let him irritate me. I don't know how to—" Her words falter.

Raqia sighs. "I don't think his fighting with you will turn him, if that's what's worrying you."

Anabelle looks unsure about that but then shrugs to

slough off their tension. "Well, we're not going to solve this problem right now." She puts on a wan smile. "We have a dance to get ready for."

Raqia nods but knows they are only putting it aside for the moment.

They're both still applying their make-up when Eddie's footsteps clomp down the hallway and he bangs on Anabelle's bedroom door. She puts her head in her hands and mumbles, "I'm not ready for him yet." Then she calls out, "Go away, Eddie."

"No."

"It's not a big deal," Raqia says. "We're already dressed."

"Fine," Anabelle says. She darts around to find her cat, then picks him up and holds him to her chest. "Come in," she calls, her voice strained as Chuy struggles to escape her vise-like embrace.

Eddie bursts through the door—then stops short. "You two match." The look on his face suggests he doesn't know what to think of that.

"What do you want?" Anabelle scowls as Chuy bats at her neck, paws tangling in her hair.

"I brought you these." He holds out two large magnolia flowers, one for each of them. The stems are freshly severed, still smell like the tree in their backyard.

"Aw, that's sweet," Raqia says. A smile blooms up from inside her; she doesn't even care that there isn't any way she can wear the thing. The lemony bloom is the size of her face and looks like suede. She's careful not to touch the petals, so their creamy beauty won't turn brown.

"Last of the season," he says. Raqia notices he's shaved, again.

"Thanks," Anabelle mutters. She has to let go of her cat to take the flower, and Chuy scampers off into the hall.

Now Eddie looks pointedly at Raqia and her thick cascade of waves. Taita helped her style her hair like a 1930s screen siren. "No braid tonight?"

She grins. "Do you like it?"

He just nods slowly, his expression guarded. Does he really like it? She can't tell. He stares at her a little longer then turns toward the mirror on the back of the door, straightens the emerald silk tie he has loosely knotted around the open collar of his crisp navy dress shirt. He tucks his chin-length hair behind one ear; it's only a little neater than usual. Polished and rakish. The combination looks…good.

Anabelle blots her pink lip gloss as she slips on her heels. When she stands, she wobbles.

"Are you nuts?" her brother asks her reflection, his extra niceness suddenly evaporating. "Your shoes are six inches tall! How are you going to dance in them?"

"They're only four-and-a-quarter," she snaps back as she clasps on a necklace with a gold cross pendant. "And who knows if I *will* dance, since you scared off my date."

"No great loss there." He turns back to face her. "I

don't want you going out with some dumb bunny weakling. If he's not man enough to be around your brother, you're better off without him." Then he looks at Raqia. "No mousy boys vying for *your* attentions tonight, are there?"

As if, she thinks but just shakes her head.

The doorbell rings. Anabelle glares at Eddie as she stalks shakily past and down the hall. He smiles at Raqia, who just shakes her head as she falls into step close behind his sister, ready to put out her hand if needed. Anabelle is liable to break an ankle tonight, assuming she even makes it downstairs.

"You look like a newborn giraffe," Eddie calls out.

Anabelle spins dangerously around, her eyes wide with a mixture of hope and annoyance. "Really?" she challenges. He just shrugs. Her eyes narrow and she turns back to continue down the steps. Raqia shoots Eddie a warning look—she doesn't want to play referee tonight—and he holds his hands up in a "who, me?" gesture.

Their mom is letting a small group into the foyer. Three couples, Eddie's friends from Thursday night and their girlfriends, file in next to Puppyface, who already stands waiting by the entrance to the dining room. The boys make woots and hollers at Eddie, calling him "The Wolf" as he descends the stairs with his cocky grin.

"Oh, yay," Anabelle deadpans. "The fan club." While they all stand around in the hall, waiting for Mrs. Foster to get her camera, the boys ignore their dates in favor of chatting up their idol. Puppyface appears to be going stag—no surprise there. He edges toward Raqia, cocks his head and stares at her with those unsettling ice-blue eyes.

Anabelle wedges herself between them. "What's the matter? You seem to be staring at Rocky." Before he can respond, she says, "Quit it. It's gross." Her smile is as pleasant as ice cream after church on Sunday, but her point is clear.

"I can look at her if I want to."

"You do that," Anabelle says quietly. "But if it bothers her, you can be sure Eddie will rip out your throat." She smiles again.

His complexion turns as cold as his eyes, then, and he grudgingly turns back to Eddie.

"Thank you," Raqia murmurs to Anabelle, who squeezes her hand briefly.

She whispers back, "If any wolf packs do turn up in Houston, my guess is his creepy mug will be the first one on the news."

Raqia and Anabelle don't know the other girls, who stand shoulder to shoulder in a defensive line. Their short tank dresses are mostly obscured behind homecoming mums: a particularly Texan tradition that celebrates each wearer's Affinity with profusions of fake flowers, craft store decorations, and polyester ribbons streaming all the way to their feet. The mums have to be held up with halter straps around the girls' necks like the world's ugliest aprons.

One of the monstrosities has two teddy bears on it, holding hands and kissing against the backdrop of a gawdy valentine heart—a display inspired, Raqia thinks, by its wearer's small glassy eyes, tiny nose, and rounded ears. One of the other mums lights up with twinkling colored lights in the shape of a butterfly, and the third's leopard print ribbons all end in tinny bells that clink every time the girl wearing them takes a step and her feet bang against them.

Forget Anabelle's trouble walking, Raqia thinks. She's sure one of these girls will trip on her mum's tails before the night is over.

The butterfly girl rests her hands on her hips and flexes her arms back and forth. "Where's your mum?" she asks, looking Anabelle up and down. The leopard ribbon girl pretends to inspect her long black nails, but she's watching Anabelle out of the corner of her eye.

"Her date couldn't be here," Raqia says, heading off an uncomfortable conversation about their lack of Affinity. She nudges Anabelle. "Your cat came downstairs earlier. Do you want to tell him good-bye?"

She gives her a grateful look. "Yes, he'll be sad if I don't." Raqia doubts Chuy will care, but Anabelle's comment seems to deflect Butterfly Girl's curiosity. Anabelle shakily traipses off just as her mom comes back in to take pictures.

Mr. Foster's booming voice precedes him into the hallway. "Fantastic game last night, men!" A boisterous cacophony of cheering and chuckling and reliving the favorite plays of the game crowds Raqia and the other girls right out of the hall. Raqia perches up on the staircase. Mr. Foster has one arm around Eddie and another around Puppyface and is telling a story about when *he* was the star quarterback in high school. Eddie looks uncomfortable and glances at Raqia, who just shrugs. If Eddie isn't used to this by now, he never will be.

Raqia can't relate.

Mrs. Foster looks like she's having a wonderful time. "I love that you wear the mums all weekend!" she gushes. "It seems a shame to have them only on game night." One of the fanboys mutters in agreement, alluding to how expensive the mums are. Mrs. Foster points to the teddy bears approvingly. "So elaborate!" Then she makes every couple line up for a picture in the archway leading to the dining room. After that, she waves Raqia and Anabelle over. They stand there and smile to be polite, but Anabelle is still miffed about being stood up, and Raqia just feels vaguely uncomfortable, even without some craft store crime scene around her neck. Mrs. Foster turns to her son. "Here, Eddie, come get in the picture with them."

He bounds over and puts an arm around each of them. Anabelle groans but still cooperates. In that moment, all three of them standing arm in arm, Raqia thinks of all the first day of school pictures they've had together in this hallway, and for the space of a shutter click, they are the same kids they were, the camera's flash burning away the tension between them.

As everyone gets ready to leave, Puppyface positions himself next to Raqia, as close as a shadow. She steps away from him toward Anabelle, and Eddie notices. His glance sharpens toward Puppyface as he shakes his head slowly. A subtle gesture, but it's enough; Puppyface moves back.

"You guys have fun tonight," Mr. Foster says, opening the front door. As everyone files out toward their respective cars, Mr. Foster puts a hand on Eddie's shoulder. "Be careful, son," he says quietly. "Dinner and dance, then back home." He catches Raqia's eye for the space of a second, and she raises her eyebrows.

"Don't worry, Dad." Eddie ushers his sister out the door then turns back. "You coming, Rocky?"

Raqia nods and follows, as Mrs. Foster switches the television onto one of the news channels. Dr. Crystalle Delacourt's resonant voice echoes into the hallway—another plea for volunteers for her study on wolf Affinities—as the front door closes behind them.

5

BY THE time they reach the Italian restaurant, Eddie's friends are getting on Raqia's nerves with their fawning over him and their complete disregard of their girlfriends.

Julie, Kirstin, and Nala—whose names Raqia learned only once they arrived at the restaurant because their dates have zero manners—seem more intent on making sure they don't get pasta sauce on their mums than actually eating very much. One of them has pushed her plate away entirely, deciding she will have nothing but breadsticks.

They keep to themselves at one end of the long table, and Raqia sits with Anabelle at the other end, digging into some delicious chicken fettuccini alfredo and avoiding any mention of Affinities. The guys are making enough noise, clustered around Eddie in the middle of the group, that Raqia couldn't make conversation with their dates even if she wanted to.

"They look kind of ridiculous," she murmurs, pointing at Julie's intricate ballet of teddy bear avoidant spaghetti.

Anabelle grunts in response, but then a dollop of marinara sauce plops down onto Julie's mum.

"Oh no!" Kirstin squeals and begins rubbing Julie's sauce-covered stuffed animal vigorously with her napkin until it looks like a zombie bear.

"You're only making it worse!" Nala says, dipping her own napkin into her seltzer and trying to help clean the marinara sauce away. Julie looks like she wants to cry. Their dates are just staring at them.

"Those mums are a macabre farce. Bet you're glad not to be wearing one now, aren't you?" Raqia says under her breath, and Anabelle giggle-snorts into her cola. "Am I right?" Raqia laughs quietly.

Eddie gives Raqia a sharp look, but she's had enough. "What, we aren't allowed to enjoy ourselves, too?" The others aren't paying attention, but she keeps her voice quiet because she doesn't want to embarrass him if she doesn't have to. "Every night doesn't have to be about you."

He looks stung but hides his face behind his glass of soda, and she feels sorry for making him feel bad. It isn't his fault he has a lot of friends. Raqia might be just as exuberant if she had a table full of people excited about the things she had to say, too. She would even wear any stupid mum if she were entitled to do so.

As he drinks, Anabelle frowns at them, questions in her eyes, but Raqia just waves the conversation away and goes back to her pasta.

A few minutes later, when Eddie switches places with one of his fanboys to sit next to Raqia, Anabelle stands sharply and excuses herself to the restroom. Eddie watches his friends engrossed in their own conversation for a minute, then he leans over to Raqia and asks, "If I tell you something, can you keep it quiet?"

"What, you mean like a secret?" Raqia looks around the table; no one else is paying attention to them for a moment. "Was Puppyface involved in the liquor store robbery this morning?"

He scowls. "Who? No, I don't know who did that. Some jackass giving us a bad name."

"Are you thinking about participating in that study on wolf Affinities?"

Now he grimaces. "No, *thank* you. That's not the kind of attention I want."

"Look, Eddie, I know that you're not the kind of wolf likely to get his mugshot on the news. At least, I hope you aren't," she adds.

"Seriously? You think I would be involved with that stuff?" He shakes his head. "I'm trying to make sure it doesn't—" He exhales loudly. "Never mind. That's not what I wanted to talk about." He lowers his voice even more, so Raqia has to bend close to hear him. "I'm thinking about transferring to another school. There are some stellar engineering programs here at home, and let's face it, even as good as I am, the chances I make a pro roster are zero to none." He flicks a crust of bread off the table. "As if anyone in his right mind would even *want* to."

The bitterness in his tone surprises Raqia. "I thought you loved football."

"I did. And being competent at it made a lot of things easier for me. But I want more."

Raqia snorts into her cola. "*More?* Greedy much?"

"That's not what I meant. More out of life."

Raqia nods. She understands that feeling well.

He leans closer to her. "Look, I don't want to play for the NFL; I want a Ph.D. and a career that means something. I want a family—and I don't want to be traveling around, chasing a stupid ball, all the time. Science is going to win out over sports. I refuse to be pigeoned."

Just then Puppyface laughs too loudly at something one of the other guys has said and draws the attention of several tables around them. Raqia thinks maybe *he* ought to sign up for Dr. Delacourt's research study; he seems like someone who would benefit from rigorous oversight. Eddie glares at him until he quiets down, then he murmurs, "I need to be here." Once Puppyface has blended back into the tamer conversation of the table, Eddie adds, "Here. Not in some provincial college town. I want to show the world there's more to me than a wolf."

"So you'd come back home." Raqia grins. "Anabelle would love that."

He rolls his eyes. "Whatever. I have more important things to deal with than her drama."

She feels indignant on Anabelle's behalf, but only a

little. Then a more serious thought occurs to her. "If you transfer, you would lose your scholarship." Mr. Foster will be furious. Maybe Dr. Delacourt's study will pay—but even if it does, that won't be enough for college tuition.

Eddie nods. "It's a problem," he admits. "I need some time still to figure it out. I feel stuck."

Before Raqia can say anything else, Anabelle is back. "Stuck how?" she asks, sliding into her chair.

Eddie just shrugs and says, "Nothing. It doesn't matter."

"Come on, tell me," Anabelle says. "You told Rocky."

"Just forget about it," he says. Raqia doesn't like the way Anabelle glares at her for just a moment, as if *she* has done something wrong.

"What, are you *his* best friend now?" she mutters under her breath, but Raqia hears it, calling out to her like a siren through the ambient noise of the restaurant. Anabelle doesn't look up from her food, so Raqia pretends not to notice. She doesn't want to fight.

Eddie's ears perk up, like he heard his sister too, but then he starts making half-hearted jokes with the guy sitting next to him. Otherwise he and Anabelle both seem subdued through the rest of dinner, and Raqia eats every last bite of pasta off her huge plate just to fill the time until it's over.

6

AS SOON as they get to the dance, the three couples scatter into the streamers and balloons, the boys high-fiving Eddie on their way into the crowd. One of the football coaches comes up and greets Eddie with some warmth, acknowledging Anabelle and Raqia tangentially, and asks about the team Eddie is playing on now. Raqia looks past the foyer into the dance. Everyone in the dimly lit gym seems to belong together. When the coach walks away, Puppyface, who has been on good behavior for the last hour or so, admits he's been angling for more time on the field and goes after him.

Several more people arrive in the foyer then and file past them into the dance. A couple of girls, seniors Raqia knows only by sight, stop to lavish their squealing greetings on Eddie, who accepts them with friendly distance, holding one at actual arms' length when she tries to hug him. She looks surprised, and when Eddie takes a step closer to Raqia, she looks at her as if Raqia were a bug.

"Where's your mum?" the senior asks, her gaze taking all of Raqia in as if she has eight eyes.

Raqia doesn't know how to answer. Isn't it obvious? She has no Affinity and no date to give her a mum even if she'd matured yet—

Eddie scoffs. "She doesn't need one. Those crazy things look absurd."

This catches Anabelle's attention. She focuses on the conversation suddenly as if she were being left out of something important. "Well, there *was* that enormous magnolia. Not that there was any way to wear it. But who needs a mum when you have a flower as big as your head?" She gives Eddie a pointed look, then shifts it to Raqia.

The other senior puts a hand on her friend's arm. "Let's just go into the dance," she says, pulling her away. Too-many-eyes walks off with her reluctantly.

Eddie is standing so close Raqia can smell, for the first time, the subtle notes of his cologne. Did he mean to imply he was here as her date? *No way.* But the way Anabelle is looking at the two of them…she clearly must be wondering the same thing.

"What?" he asks his sister, defensiveness lurking in his tone.

"That was ridiculous. Raqia doesn't need you to—" Anabelle shakes her head and sways on her shoes. "You don't play here anymore. Let it go."

Eddie turns to face her head-on. "You weren't complaining last year when my popularity upped your street cred." His voice is even but his eyes, fierce. "I think you're jealous."

Anabelle grits her teeth. "Your charm has worn off."

Raqia steps between them and puts a hand on each of their arms. "Maybe you could save this fight for tomorrow? There's a lotta people here—"

"And you don't want me to *wolf out* in front of them, do you." But he's staring at his sister.

Anabelle flinches first, screwing up her nose and eyes. *"Aarrgghh!"* She pivots and wobble-stomps on her toes over to the table with the snacks and begins filling up a green cocktail napkin with cheez balls.

"You shouldn't provoke her like that," Raqia says. Her hand is still on Eddie's arm; it feels tense under her fingers, and she pats him gently. "She only digs in."

He puts his hand on top of Raqia's, surprising her, but then loosens up. "I know." He smiles coolly. "Family brings out the worst in us sometimes." He leads Raqia the rest of the way into the dance. Then he looks back up at his sister, and his grin darkens.

Anabelle is talking to one of their classmates, a guy with longish ears and downy fuzz on his cheeks. *Taylor,* Raqia realizes, Anabelle's crush. *No wonder he's scared of Eddie,* she thinks, noticing that his nose quivers excitedly when he talks. Anabelle has put her cheez balls on the table and has a hand on Taylor's arm, smiling and cutting her eyes at him in a way that makes him grin from one outsized ear to the other. Raqia notes Anabelle's trembling ankle and wonders whether Taylor can see it. They make a cute couple. Just looking at them makes her feel optimistic.

"Eddie," she says, leaning closer so she won't have to shout over the music, "don't mess this up for her, please."

"What're you talking about?"

"I mean it." She tries her most stern voice. "I'll be really mad at you on her behalf."

Eddie looks down at her in surprise. "Okay, Rocky, that's fine. I won't go bust up what is, no doubt, an uninspired conversation."

Raqia nods curtly then looks back over at the pair. Taylor gestures toward the dance floor. Anabelle nods, a hopeful smile on her face. He offers her his hand as they walk into the crowd.

"But you have to dance with me to keep me occupied." Eddie pulls Raqia toward the middle of the gym just as the languid strains of a rock ballad begin. The whole place is a dark mix of silhouetted bodies and noise. Occasional colored lights flash across the room, highlighting her schoolmates' enthusiasm or embarrassment. Some whose Animal Affinities have already emerged, like the captain of the cheer squad in satin tiger-stripe pants, have dressed to emphasize their pride in the idea that they are somehow, now, more mature than everyone else.

But when the other students see Raqia and Eddie, they either gape at them or…give them a wide berth. She tries to parse out what it means that they are dancing together—nothing, of course, no matter how warm and strong his hands feel around her waist—and what other people will think it means. That's another story.

How will it change things for her at school next week, if anyone still remembers after a couple of days? Everyone knows Raqia is friends with Eddie. Or at least, anyone who has ever paid attention to her and Anabelle has seen all three of them together. Will thinking she's here with him on a date change the way people think about her? Will anyone expect Eddie to be interested in someone who might ultimately end up Plain?

She looks around at some of the other couples slow-dancing, at the cumbersome space a few of the girls' mums drive between them and their dates. Raqia feels just as awkward, even though it isn't like she's never stood this close to Eddie before. But dancing this way feels different tonight, when he seems to be acting like her date. But he isn't her date. And yet, as he turns them in a slow circle in time to the music, he draws her even closer. She shakes her head, confused by her own thoughts about what this is and what it will mean at school on Monday. She can just stay here in this moment instead, pretending she and Eddie, their arms around each other, are suspended in the midway of any ordinary hug.

A few students bound over, excited to see Eddie. He smiles, friendly and nice as ever, but doesn't stop swaying to the music with Raqia. One calls him "bunny wrecker" as if it were some incredible inside joke, and Eddie just nods, a weary smile on his face. "I am what I am," he says and shrugs.

Then they're alone again, in the middle of a crowd. "I hate that nickname," he mutters.

This surprises her. He never shied away from his reputation in high school.

"They act like it was fun to break open a living rabbit and gnaw on its raw, bleeding leg. I wasn't even thirteen, for chrissake. I had no idea what to do, how strong that urge would be." He shakes his head.

After a moment, she asks, "Do you ever wish maybe you didn't have your Affinity?" The sad—almost... pitying—look on his face makes her add, "Or that you had a different one?"

He shakes his head. "I am what I am," he murmurs, his tone somber, intimate. "The occasional savage tendency and all."

"You've managed to control yourself admirably in the years since that campout," Raqia says, trying to buoy his mood. "I've never seen you attack anything else." She smiles. "Unless you've been hiding it from us, running off to the woods under the full moon."

He actually laughs then, a quiet, comfortable sound. She loves it. "Hardly," he says.

With Eddie pacified, Raqia tries to keep one eye on Anabelle—at least if she trips on her own feet Taylor is close enough to catch her—but Eddie turns her so that her back is to them.

"Try to focus on your dance partner." He grins, but there is a thin edge to his voice that catches her attention. His hands on her waist feel strained, as if he wants to pull her closer and holding back is a difficult choice.

Trying to recapture the easy playfulness of their childhood, she reaches up and tousles his hair. "Behave, wolf boy." She smiles with a self-assurance she doesn't entirely feel.

He hesitates. "What if I don't want to?" His demeanor is serious, intent. "What would *you* think if I came back to Houston? If I stayed here." His fingers tighten at her sides just a little, then relax.

If he comes back, if he stays, will their trio form again? Right now, it feels like a lopsided triangle. Raqia wants to turn around and look at Anabelle but can't—and then she decides she doesn't really want to. She can say nothing, just hold herself in this halted moment of indecision. Maybe she can just hold Eddie, right now, for this short time, without—

When she doesn't answer, he sighs, a soft sound through his nose like a dog, resigned, settling in. His eyes wander around the room as they sway to the most doleful guitar solo she's ever heard.

It's comfortable dancing with Eddie. He has never felt

threatening, never to her, no matter how much Taita worried about it when his Affinity first came out. Even now, when he leans his head down close to hers, when his hands move closer to each other around her back, even now, she feels safe. But Anabelle's conflicted feelings toward her brother have only grown more intense—anxious, erratic—in the wake of all the recent attacks. Maybe if wolves weren't so feared then Anabelle wouldn't always be at such odds with him. But who knows how to make wolves seem like less of a threat? And if Raqia lets her friendship with Eddie slide into something deeper…which right now feels very appealing… Well, she doesn't know exactly what Anabelle will do, but it won't be pretty. How can Raqia choose between them?

Eddie's skin smells faintly of cedarwood, like the carved wooden blanket chest in her grandmother's bedroom. Cedar is Taita's favorite scent, and the cedar of Lebanon is the tree stamped on the gold pendants Taita and Raqia wear on delicate chains around their necks. Taita said they were for remembrance; hers is bound up in the memory of home and family. But Raqia's reminds her of a homeland everyone knows she is from, but that she left so long ago, her memory of it is shrouded in mountain fog. Still, she feels apart. It's like having one foot in a place she can barely remember and one in a place that hardly thinks of her.

Raqia's only early memory is from right before they emigrated. She attended a tree planting ceremony with her father in the cedar forest. His university classes were there, too, some sort of field trip. Taita held her while she threw a tiny clump of soil at the new planting. It was a ceremony meant to celebrate efforts to foster new growth in the forest, but now Raqia thinks it feels more like she was burying the dead.

As the song comes to an end, the DJ unexpectedly spins another ballad, and Raqia decides she can just keep dancing with Eddie, who seems even less tense now. They drift around and see Anabelle and Taylor on the fringe of the crowd, also swaying in a wobbly euphoria.

"She worries about you," Raqia says, "a lot."

"I know she's mad because she's still Plain."

Raqia looks up at him. "Then why pick on her so much?"

"I don't know. It's what brothers do?"

That's an unsatisfying answer. "Big brothers also look out for their little sisters—and not just by interfering with who they're dating." Eddie and Anabelle are the closest thing she's ever had to siblings. "But then what do I know," she adds in a mumble.

When she was really young, maybe nine or ten, she decided one day to adopt them as her brother and sister and proudly announced this to Taita.

Her grandmother laughed, a mirthless, high-pitched screech, and said, "Habibti, they're not really your family, no matter how much you want them to be." Taita patted Raqia's shoulder affectionately, but when she saw her granddaughter's downcast eyes and quivering lip, she said, "But of course, Anabelle is your closest friend, and of course that's *like* family." But the underlying message was that Taita was all Raqia really had. Raqia had never felt lonelier than that day.

Dancing with Eddie, his face so close to hers, the music loud and the lights low, she doesn't feel so lonely. She also doesn't feel especially sisterly.

Suddenly there's a loud crash from the back of the gym, and Raqia turns around to see one of the balloon archways has fallen down, a casualty of a fight between a couple of guys. She can't tell who they are, but it doesn't take long for three or four others to join in the scuffle; it looks like Puppyface is among them. Eddie's arm tightens around her shoulders and a low rumble forms in his chest.

She puts her hand against him. "Don't even think about it," she warns. "I don't care how much everyone loved 'The Wolf' on the football field last year, you'll be thrown out if you get aggressive here."

The eyes he turns on her are angry, distant. "You don't know what you're talking about."

"How do you think people will react if a wolf pack turns up in Houston?" she asks. "You may be popular and in control of your emotions, but you're also the most flamboyant beast this school has ever seen." She looks back at the fight. Puppyface throws a punch at someone. She points at him. "And *that guy* is one of your friends." Panic strains her voice; she reaches up to speak closer to his ear. "You were even on the news when you made All-American. Do you honestly imagine you won't be the first person people blame?" She gestures to the crowd of students, no longer dancing, now egging on the fight. "What college student comes back to his high school for a dance?" He looks intently at her then, but she can't—won't—believe he came here for her. "You have a following—the football players all think you hung the moon. Don't try to deny you love the attention."

"They're all full of shit," he growls. "They don't know me at all." But he is holding himself in check.

Refusing to be pigeoned, she thinks. He clearly wants to get involved in the mess at the other end of the room, though. Then one of his fanboys stalks past them and Eddie grabs his arm, holds him back.

His voice in his friend's ear is low but Raqia still hears it. "Think first," he warns him. "Who is that going to help?"

It occurs to her that maybe Eddie wants to curb the fight, not join it. Maybe moving back to Houston will allow him to keep the other wolves, his fanboys, in check, too.

Raqia looks back at the melee and is surprised to feel her own heat rising, the hair on the back of her neck standing up. A passel of teachers and the basketball coach are heading toward the boys to stop the brawl. The music has finally stopped.

She glances around for Anabelle and soon finds her,

holding Taylor's hand at the back edge of the crowd. He looks entertained, but Anabelle is watching her brother nervously. Raqia gives her a reassuring smile, but when she looks back at Eddie—why is he staring at *her*? Suddenly self-conscious, she rubs her arm and feels gooseflesh.

"The fight's breaking up," she says. He nods, tilts his head at her. The rest of the crowd is dispersing, too, the students wandering around the gym in clusters. Several make their way to the snack table. One of the football coaches has Puppyface off to the side, a hand on his shoulder, keeping him back out of the fray.

The noise of chatter and footsteps and laughter becomes louder than Raqia can stand, then suddenly a few voices sharpen into pinpricks of focus. She can hear the basketball coach and assistant principal reprimanding the two boys who started the fight in the first place. She can hear their weak excuses, the conversation impossibly rising above the swell of everyone else's talking. *He called me a Plain One,* the kid with the cut on his forehead is saying. *He hit me first,* says the kid with the bloody nose. Raqia can smell him, the mess of his face—

She feels lightheaded.

Eddie catches her around the small of her back. "Hang on, Rocky." She leans against him, closes her eyes. Is vaguely aware of his other arm waving.

Then Anabelle's voice, part confusion, part dismay. "But I'm not ready to leave yet."

Raqia swims up through the noise, opens her eyes. Anabelle looks pissed; Taylor hangs back, casting nervous glances at Eddie. "What? Why are we leaving?" Raqia asks, standing straight again—but slowly.

Eddie glares at her. "I'm getting you out of here."

The angry look on Anabelle's face prompts Raqia to say, "I'm fine," but then a tremor in her stomach jolts her still, and a wave of nausea hits.

"You look green," Anabelle says, her forehead wrinkling. "Is something wrong?"

"Too much pasta." Raqia's voice sounds as weak as she suddenly feels. Everything is horrible.

"Come on, home with you. Let's go, sis."

Anabelle looks back at Taylor. "But—"

"*Now,*" Eddie insists, gravel in his voice. He looks down at Raqia. "Taita'll kill me if I don't get you home when you're sick."

Taylor nods rapidly, his nose quivering as if the threat of violence were real. "See you Monday."

"No, wait—" Anabelle says but Raqia sees him back away out of the corner of her eye. As he walks away, Anabelle wails in frustration. "You ruin *everything,*" she says to her brother, who ignores her. She opens her tiny purse and holds out a small packet of stomach ache tablets. "This will help," she says to Raqia. "Why don't you take them?"

"That's not going to be enough," Eddie says. Raqia lets him lead her out of the gym, his arm steady around her.

"Aren't you even going to try it?" Anabelle insists, but he keeps walking, pulling Raqia along. Anabelle takes off her shoes so she can stomp next to them, but her bare feet can't properly convey her irritation. "Just give me five more minutes." The music in the dance starts up again. "One more song?" She bargains against their sudden departure all the way to the car.

Listening to her makes Raqia feel even worse. *Just. Stop,* she thinks. She probably has food poisoning. She's sorry Anabelle has to leave Taylor, but—then another wave of nausea roils her gut. She also wants, just a little, to slap her. The urge surprises her and makes her feel even sicker. She clenches her entire body until the churning passes. When Anabelle mutters something about "all this over indigestion," all Raqia can think is, *Whatever.*

On the way home, Eddie takes the freeway to save time, barreling down the shortcut while Anabelle complains.

"I don't see why you couldn't have let me stay at the dance. Taylor could have brought me home."

"Doubtful," Eddie says, his voice low and angry.

"Then you could have come back and picked me up—"

Eddie turns and growls at her, eyes as dark as Raqia has ever seen them. Even she quakes a little at the sound, but then suddenly she thinks she might throw up and lurches. Eddie puts a gentle hand on her shoulder.

"You're going to be okay, Rocky," he says, quiet, steady.

Anabelle starts to protest again. Raqia is ready for her

friend to embrace a little Christ-like compassion already.

Apparently so is Eddie. "You can quit bitching any time now," he finally says, his voice even, his eyes focused as he swerves onto the exit ramp and rolls through the stop signs in their neighborhood. Anabelle shuts up. Or fades out.

The darkness around the edges of Raqia's perception grows larger, consuming…

7

RAQIA DOESN'T remember going inside her house or getting into bed. She wakes up in the middle of the night, parched but no longer nauseated. She goes into the bathroom for a drink of water, but when she turns on the light, what she sees in the mirror makes her jump back against the wall with a strangled shriek.

Her skin is bruised. All over.

As her eyes adjust, blue-gray splotches come into focus on her cheeks and neck and arms and chest and legs. Dark, uneven mandalas, swirling across her skin. She touches them, gingerly. The skin doesn't feel tender. She traces the splotches and finds them to be patterns. They are more like tattoos than bruises, she realizes, but where the hell have they come from?

She opens her mouth to call for Taita, but her voice has vanished. She strains her throat, pushing all the air in her lungs out into a hollow, faint scream that sends her spinning into fear. She claws at her skin as the bruises swallow her up, she grasps at the air, clutches at her own reflection in the mirror, then spins and twists off her balance, falling,

falling, her throat screaming into silence—

She darts straight up in her bed, sweating and panting and whimpering, the covers tangled around her. Her pillows have been tossed to the floor. She stares at her skin, her perfect olive skin, no blemishes anywhere.

No bruises. No mandalas. No freckles, even. Everything as smooth and soft as ever, but with a thin sheen of sweat. Her body is still heaving from what must have been a nightmare, the most surreal dream she's ever had.

She reaches for her phone to send Anabelle a text. **something weird happened**, she types.

Three little flashing dots indicate Anabelle is typing, then they vanish. A moment later, the dots again, but then nothing. Finally, a text comes through.

are you still sick?

She doesn't feel nauseated anymore, just unsettled. **I don't think so.**

The three dots again, then they vanish. Appear, and vanish. *What* is going on with Anabelle?

Raqia texts once more. **call me?**

The response comes less than a minute later. **no thanks. I thought you were my friend.**

Raqia feels stunned. All this because Eddie made her leave the dance early? It's not as if Raqia *tried* to ruin her night—or as if Anabelle won't see Taylor at school. They have three classes together! She types, **I don't understand.**

`sure you don't.` An eye-roll emoji. `nothing is the same. not anymore. it can't be.`

Bypassing any twinge of remorse, Raqia rockets straight into anger. She didn't mean to get sick, the nightmare terrified her, she's confused enough about Eddie—*she* deserves to be the most important person in her concern, not Anabelle. She looks down at her arms, legs, chest, confirms her skin is normal.

"So weird," she mutters, suddenly so tired. Picking up her pillows makes her dizzy.

She thinks about waking Taita up but can't muster the energy. She should sleep. *All* of this has to be a dream, an insane, sick-person dream. When she wakes up tomorrow, she insists to herself, everything will be normal again. She fades back into sleep in a second.

8

RAQIA SLEEPS so late on Sunday that Taita is already making lunch by the time she comes downstairs.

"How are you feeling, habibti?" she asks, concern tracked across her brow.

"Better than last night, I guess." The dream didn't come back, but that didn't stop Raqia from thoroughly inspecting her body when she woke up for the discolorations she imagined in her sick state in the middle of the night. The text messages were real, however. Anabelle's last one is still displayed on her phone; she hasn't sent another this morning, even though Raqia has tried to contact her more than once. "Was I in bad shape when I got home?"

Taita looks up sharply from the shredded chicken and rice she is stirring. "You don't remember? Eddie had to help me get you into your room." She shakes her head and begins folding sautéed crumbles of ground lamb and pine nuts into the dish. "I'd have thought you'd been drinking alcohol if I didn't know you better." She cuts her eyes at Raqia above her glasses.

"None of us had anything to drink but soda." Raqia sniffs the aroma.

"Do you promise?"

Raqia can't mask her surprise. "When have I ever drunk alcohol?" Truly, she has no interest in anything that makes her feel sick and foggy and act like a brainless boar. Anabelle is too religious to touch the stuff, so Raqia never has any social pressure to imbibe.

"I suppose that's true." Taita appears to relax.

"Are you making hashwe?" she asks. Taita smiles and nods. "That smells really good." Raqia's stomach rumbles. "I hope we eat soon."

After lunch, she inspects herself in the mirror before she showers. No markings. By the time she gets dressed and finishes braiding her wet hair, Eddie calls.

"How you feeling today?" he asks, his voice low and serious.

"Okay, I guess."

"Any more…weird symptoms?"

That's an odd question. "Just a totally surreal nightmare." But describing it will sound crazy. "No big deal." Dismissing it diminishes it.

"Okay, well…good." He clears his throat. "I'm glad you're feeling better."

"Yeah." More or less. Better enough. "So is Anabelle really mad at me?"

He snorts. "She'll get over it."

What can she be mad about? And is it the kind of mad that will wreck their friendship? Raqia can't decide whether the situation is more unnerving or ludicrous. She needs to talk to her in person. "Is she home? I want to come over."

Eddie's voice brightens. "Fine with me! Come on by."

When Raqia arrives, Anabelle is sulking in her bedroom, holding her unwilling cat and listening to music through her earbuds.

Eddie stands in the doorway and smirks. "She's communing with God over there," he says. "God-music in her ears, the god-cat in her lap. Probably trying to figure out how to be more godly." He leans forward and waves his hand to get her attention. When she looks at him, he says loudly, "You can start by not being a horse's ass to the one close friend who still puts up with you." He looks pointedly at Raqia. "Good luck. I have to pack. I'm heading back to school this afternoon." Then he disappears into his own room down the hall.

"Hey," Raqia says, sitting on the bed. Her friend just stares at her, doesn't even take out her earbuds. A sudden flash of worry spreads through her, heating her from the inside then making her feel suddenly cold.

Even when they've gotten into arguments in the past, about what music to listen to in the car or what movie to go see, Anabelle has never seemed truly angry. Well, there was that one time Raqia told her she didn't enjoy going to

Anabelle's church, and Anabelle didn't speak to her for three days, until she went back to church and got filled up with Christ's love again and then forgave Raqia for her sinful attitude.

You know what? Raqia thinks. *That wasn't fair, either.*

"I said, hey," Raqia says more loudly, reaching over to pull Anabelle's earbuds out. A miniature Christian rock concert comes pouring out and for some reason the sound pisses her off.

Anabelle huffs and turns her back to Raqia. Chuy tries to scramble over her shoulder to get away, but Anabelle holds firm.

"Why're you upset?" Raqia can feel her temperature rising again. She hopes it isn't a fever. "I'm sorry I got sick at the dance, if that's what you want to hear. It's not like I did it on purpose."

"Yeah, *sick,*" Anabelle says.

Raqia can feel a wide gulf opening between them, one she can't hope to reach across. Not anymore.

Suddenly everything feels swimmy. She puts her hand out to the bedpost to steady herself. "I didn't want you to have to leave. But Eddie—"

"*Aarggh!* I *hate* him."

"Fine, but don't be mad at *me*!"

Anabelle turns around and—stares at Raqia with revulsion, like some awful thing she's never seen before. Raqia looks down to find the bruises, real this time, slowly darkening. She can't feel them. They're blooming onto her skin beneath the hem of her skirt, she sees them when she peeks inside her t-shirt. They're *real*. Her first impulse is to panic; she starts sweating.

"Eddie!" Anabelle shrieks. She jumps up and Chuy leaps away from her. "Get in here!" Anabelle looks like she wants to put out her hand toward Raqia but then—stops. She folds her arms up tight and refuses to come any closer. "I can't believe you," she says to her, her voice no longer scared but furious.

Eddie comes in quickly, just as Raqia feels like she's falling, and steadies her. "Yeah, I thought so," he says, helping her to sit on the edge of Anabelle's bed. "Hang on, Rocky, you're going to be okay."

She looks up at him through a fog. He keeps telling her that, but how can he know?

"Shh, don't worry," he says and pulls up his sleeve. There, on his skin, are the same blue-gray mandalas that are appearing on hers.

She wants to scream but her voice comes out in a squeak. "How have I never seen those before? Why do I have them?"

"Don't be an idiot," Anabelle says, digging Chuy out from under her bed and clinging to him. "It means you're a wolf, too."

"Just because you're still Plain doesn't give you the right to be pissed at her," Eddie snaps. "No one chooses this, or when it happens." He turns to Raqia. "It's not common. It's only started happening recently, in our generation, and not very often. We don't know why yet." He shrugs, a little helplessly. "They only appear the first time, and then…when other wolves are around. Mine turned up again last night—I saw them after I took you home." How is it he looks sheepish now? "And then I convinced myself it must have been because of the fight. One of the guys must be—" He sighs. "This is flimsy." Then he looks back at her eyes. "I'm sorry, I should have called, to warn you, but I didn't want to wake you up."

"And what about the sickness?" Raqia's voice feels like she's pushing it through a strainer. "Did you feel that too? Is it normal to get so sick when your Affinity emerges?" She hasn't heard about that before, but maybe—

Eddie shakes his head slowly, wiping away a hopefulness Raqia didn't realize she's been feeling.

"It's not normal at all," Anabelle says, judgment seeping through. "Affinities aren't a sickness." She sniffs. "Well, *good* ones aren't." Anabelle clutches her cat tighter until it hisses and swipes at her face and jumps out of her arms. She touches the scratch on her cheek as the cat flees, and her eyes fill with tears. "Get out of my room," she says, her voice low and hurt, "both of you."

Eddie helps Raqia to her feet—she feels steadier now—and pulls her by the hand to leave. "There's no talking sense to her," he says.

"No," Raqia says, snatching her hand away from him. "You tell me now what your problem is, Anabelle."

"Today? It's *you.*"

Raqia's brain feels numb though her skin tingles. A fever is on her, she really is burning from the inside. She stares at the mandalas all over her body, growing ever more pronounced, larger, bleeding into each other. Then fine, soft hairs sprout from them, downy fur covering her skin, itching under her clothes. She touches her face gingerly; the "peach fuzz" she's always had is growing thicker, longer. Her fingernails seem longer, too. More shapely. Fierce.

Anabelle keeps staring at her. Eddie is tensed, ready to pounce if needed. Raqia can hear both their heartbeats.

"I don't think we can be friends anymore," Anabelle says. Her lip is shaking, her eyes filling up. "Wolves are dangerous." She glares pointedly at Eddie even as her tears start to fall. "They take things that don't belong to them. They hurt people."

Surely she doesn't think he took *me?* But then Raqia realizes it doesn't matter. Anabelle is Plain and jealous and doesn't care. Maybe it's time *she* doesn't care, either.

Suddenly filled with rage, Raqia runs from the room, runs past Eddie, who is following her, runs down the stairs. Anabelle slams her bedroom door behind them, crying loudly now. Ears ringing and her vision cloudy, Raqia nearly trips over Chuy hiding in the curve of the bottom step.

That cat is never going to help Anabelle find herself. Raqia can hear the rhythmic thump of its heart, can smell its bones and blood and tendons, can almost taste the dander of its fur in the air. That cat will never be what Anabelle wants, no matter how much she tries to make it so.

Feeling feral, unstoppable, Raqia scoops the animal up and crushes it in an embrace. The thing hisses as it jerks away from her, lets out a long, angry screech and scratches at Raqia's chin, but she squeezes it, growling in her chest—a sound that terrifies her with its vibration and timbre—as if crushing the cat can drain her fury and fear.

Then suddenly amidst the howling and hissing and unmooring power in Raqia's hands there is Eddie. He's pulling Raqia's arms open, shoving Chuy out of the way. The cat escapes in a frenzy of claws and torn fur and scratchy yowls and then Raqia's arms are crushing Eddie, and she's screaming.

"Shh, Rocky, you're okay, you're safe."

She can hear his voice, but how, *how* can he be right? She wants to shred and bite and wreck—is this a Big Bad instinct? Is that what's making her feel sick? Every cell in her body screeches and howls at the overwhelming confusion of mind and body, of lurid thought and destructive impulse.

Eddie holds her shoulders firmly, keeping her from moving until she looks into his face. He's blurry, his dark eyes intense and wavering at the same time; her cheeks feel wet and she realizes she's sobbing. She stills herself, trying to even out her breaths, trying to keep the noise in.

Eddie smiles. "There we go." He keeps one firm hand on her shoulder, and the other soothes away her tears. "Trust me, killing a small animal isn't the way you want to start this off."

She knows instinctively this both is and isn't a joke. In spite of the maelstrom inside her, she laughs, a choking sound spinning the violence down, her fear being strangled by the absurd.

"Besides, we don't want Anabelle to think her god-cat is only mortal, do we?" He's still grinning, smoothing her hair and her fury at the same time.

Raqia feels her gut clench and wants to vomit. Her throat is dry, burning. She rasps, "It was—an accident." Wasn't it? She can't actually kill something. Can she? But she wasn't able to stop herself. She looks up the stairs at the door to Anabelle's bedroom, can hear its slam re-sounding in her head, can hear Anabelle crying through the door. She looks at Eddie again, his dark eyes intense and infinite as mystery. How does he manage all of this? Is it the same for him? What keeps him from *turning?*

Eddie puts his arm around her shoulders. "Come on, I'll take you home."

What will Taita think? What will she *do?* Her grandmother has given up everything, everything but Raqia, to protect her. How can she face her? Raqia feels the soft hair that has sprung out of her, that already feels thinner, finer than it did in Anabelle's bedroom, and the nausea she felt last night starts to bubble back up.

"Don't worry, I'll talk to her with you."

Taita likes Eddie, probably even loves him, but as she so firmly pointed out, he isn't family.

Raqia wants to hide herself. "Do you have a hoodie I can wear?"

He touches her cheek lightly with the backs of his fingers, and she shivers. "You don't need one," he says. "This'll go away soon." He nods his head toward the front door. "Come on." He smiles down at her. "Trust me."

She swallows hard and takes slow, deep breaths until the nausea subsides. She lets him lead her out of the house and down the driveway, but the whole time she keeps trying to find herself in what she's just done to Anabelle's cat. Was that her? She can't understand—what *is* she now?

And Eddie—she stops and looks at him. Something in his gaze both comforts and unsettles her.

"Everything's going to be fine, Rocky, I promise."

She thinks about Anabelle and feels another wave of sick. The balance of—what is left of—their trio has shifted forever, but she can't tell whether Eddie is oblivious to this fact or triumphant in it. He pulls her along.

She takes a deep breath. She isn't Plain. She has an Affinity and...power. She can feel it vibrating inside of her, singing in her blood. She thinks of the way people react to Eddie; what will they say about *her*—what will they think now? Will she feel like she belongs—belongs to what? She startles herself by imagining her newly sharp fingernails shredding Ramón's coxcomb right off his head.

She stops short, and Eddie halts. "What is it?"

"I need to talk to Anabelle." This is not the way she wants their friendship to end. She doesn't want it to end at all.

He shakes his head. "I don't think that's wise right now."

"But—"

"Later. Give yourself time." He glances back up at the house to Anabelle's window. "Give her time, too." He looks into Raqia's eyes then. His own are dark and fiery and swallowing all at the same time. "Now let's get you home."

She stands very still until every dizzy, swimmy feeling has passed. Taita will have to understand. Then she remembers what Taita said: *I don't know, habibti… These wolves today are not like the wolves I knew… Back then, a wolf and a lamb could still be friends.*

Raqia doesn't want to believe she has Big Bad tendencies. She can show Taita that things will be all right, that wolves are more than what people see on television—although Raqia recognizes she is going to need Eddie's help for that. She can still make Taita proud of her, surely. There *has* to be a way.

She hopes she isn't being naïve.

A violent montage of the past weeks' news bulletins flashes through her mind at that moment, but she squelches them hard until everything inside of her is quiet, still, dark. She can study them later.

Actually, yes, she *can*.

But not now. *One thing at a time,* she thinks.

As she and Eddie travel across the street together, she traces the expanding mandalas on her forearm beneath the fur growing out of them and shivers, filled with terror and delight.

ACKNOWLEDGEMENTS

There are many, many people who deserve acknowledgement any time I step foot on the path to publication. For *Homecoming*, I especially want to give thanks to…

…my editor Jayne Pillemer, who has shown the world of Animal Affinities incredible love and insight…

…my critique partners Tanya Aydelott, Babette Hale, Adam Holt, Jamie Portwood, Shirley Redwine, and Emily Wagner, who are absolutely tremendous to work with…

…my critique partners David Jón Fuller and Sarah Warburton, without whom I could not possibly be the writer I am, and without whom I would have leaped from the Writer Brain ™ ledge long ago…

…my friends Brenda Leibling-Goldberg, Meredith Moore, Jenny Waldo, and the late Lucie Scott-Smith, for their insight into and enthusiasm for this manuscript in its various early stages of development…

…my friend Grant Caplan, for answering my random text messages about whether my memory of colloquial French was completely outdated…

…my friends Christa Forster, Melissa Huckabay, Kara Masharani, and Mary Meyerson, for generally being completely excellent and for their kind support in a variety of ways…

…my supportive and loving family, Aaron and Hannah and Liam, who make it possible for me to be an author because they believe in me even more than I manage to believe in myself, and that is such a gift…

…my readers, for showing the world of Animal Affinities, and all of my work, so much love over the years.

BOOK GROUP DISCUSSION QUESTIONS

1. What do you imagine the ramifications would be for killing someone's pet in a world where people have Animal Affinities? What if this pet had nothing to do with their Affinity? What could be a case for and a case against there being any consequences for such an action?

2. *Homecoming* is set in an obviously fantastical environment, yet it bears some resemblance to our own. What features of the world of Animal Affinities echo real life? What struggles that the characters face in this story could be issues real people in our own lives struggle with?

3. If you could have an Animal Affinity, what would you want it to be? What advantages would it give you? How might it cause difficulty in your life?

4. To be "other" is, very simply, to be different from the people around you in a way that causes you to feel set apart. This marker of difference, or otherness, is typically imposed rather than adopted: essentially, a person who

feels "othered" is not usually othered by choice. In what ways is Raqia made to feel like an "other" in her community? In what ways does she belong?

5. In what ways do we navigate changes in the relationships in our own lives? How do we sometimes fail? How are we sometimes successful?

6. How much of our behavior is part of our inherited characteristics (our nature) rather than what we learn (how we are nurtured)? What role does instinct play in our choices? Can we control our natural impulses? What does it cost us to do so? If we had Animal Affinities, how might we exercise self-control over our Affinities to make life meaningful?

Recently I was asked to give a speech to the members of my school community on the subject of respect. Our school goes from PreK through 12th grade, so my audience was going to be very large and would range in age from four years old to grandparent. What follows is what I said to my school community that morning.

Good morning. Thank you for inviting me here to speak about our core value of respect. This morning I'd like to tell you all a story.

When I was seven years old, my mother and my grandmother began teaching me how to cook. My grandmother, whom I called Taita because that's the Levantine Arabic word for Grandma, would come over to our house every Saturday, and she and my mother would spend the day making Lebanese food. When I was seven, they decided it was time I start learning how to do it, too. Now, learning to make Lebanese food is not a quick or simple process. There are no written recipes involved, and it takes most of the day; for example, making a batch of pita bread takes about five hours.

And while we made the food, Taita and my mother told me stories. I learned about how our family's recipes had evolved over the generations, brought from Tripoli and Zouth-n-Kayek, from Bekfiya and Beirut, then to San Antonio and finally to Houston. I learned about the many people in my family who'd made this food before me and what their lives were like. I learned Taita had not had to measure a single ingredient since the age of twelve because she'd made cooking for her large family a big part of her life's work.

And while I mixed ground lamb and onions and pine nuts to make kibbe, or stuffed grapeleaves and yellow squash with lamb and rice, I learned I was part of a rich and beautiful tradition. In learning to make this food, I came to understand my place in my family, in my culture, and—I thought—in the world.

One Monday morning, I decided to take some of the delicious Lebanese food I'd made to school with me for lunch. At that time, schools didn't worry about food allergies, so my second-grade classmates and I all traded food in the lunchroom every day. As soon as everyone sat down at a table, the negotiations would begin:

"I'll trade you a ham-and-cheese for your cupcake."

"If I give you my Cheetos, can I have half your peanut butter and jelly sandwich?"

Things like that.

Well, I'd packed my Wonder Woman lunchbox that morning with some of my favorite foods, foods I was proud of, that I had made myself while participating in my family's heritage. I started with the cookies. I asked, "Would anyone like a ma'amoul? No? I also have graybeh." They looked at me like I was speaking Martian, not Arabic. So I switched to the English names: "How about a date finger?"

There was similar disinterest for my entrée, spinach pies. These are warm hand-held pies made of soft bread and filled with spinach and onions and lemon, and they were my favorite lunch. I'd brought two because I was sure someone else would want one.

Most of the reactions to my lunch ranged from un-kindness—my classmates calling my food weird and gross—to polite distaste. They declined to sample any of it, much less trade me their Oreos for it, even though none of them had ever tried these foods before. And I felt torn: on the one hand, it looked like I was going to get to enjoy it all myself without having to share it; on the other hand, my seven-year-old sense of identity had become wrapped up in this food, in the communal process of cre-ating it, and in what it meant to be Lebanese and to be part of my family. This food represented my culture, my accomplishments, and who I was as a person. So when my friends said my lunch was weird and gross, it felt like they were saying *I* was weird and gross.

Now, I mentioned that some of them were polite. They didn't insult my lunch, but they didn't want to try it, ei-ther. Politeness *looks* like respect, but it is not the *same* as respect. If you look up respect in the dictionary, you'll see it means "to consider something in high regard." To re-spect someone or something means that you think that person or thing is important and has value. If you look up politeness in the dictionary, you'll find it means "marked by an *appearance* of deference or courtesy." Some of my classmates politely declined to share my food, but it felt like they didn't want to share in my experience, in who I was.

I did have one brave friend who, after she saw me eating my lunch, decided she would try it. She asked me if she could have a graybeh, which is a thick butter-and-sugar cookie with half a walnut embedded in the top, and I gave her one, and she liked it. Then I broke a ma'amoul – which is a sweet crumbly pastry filled with spiced dates and rolled in sugar – and gave her half. She liked that as well. She even had part of a spinach pie and declared it to be "actually pretty good." She shared her chocolate bar with me, too. That one friend showed me respect by appreciating what I had to offer.

I want to paraphrase something my wise friend Christa Forster once told me, which is that all the things which make up who we are—our memories, our traditions, what we like or value—these things which make us unique and special are all golden. And when we share what matters to us with each other, we share that gold. And when we accept other people with an open mind and an open heart, when we celebrate what makes each other unique and special, we become richer. Just like my friend in second grade who discovered a whole new cuisine she liked eating, when we respect other people by accepting them, we gain a richer understanding and appreciation of them and what they have to offer, and also of the world.

Thank you so much for your attention today. Have a wonderful school year.

Angélique Jamail
August 23, 2019

Hello!

I hope you enjoyed reading *Homecoming*. There is no greater honor for me as a writer than to know that a reader has appreciated my work. And if this story has left you with a good impression, it would be wonderful karma for you to tell others about it and to share your enjoyment of it on social media.

There is also no greater support you can give an author than your word-of-mouth recommendation, so please do share your enthusiasm! It would mean so much to me if you would leave a review for *Homecoming* on any book review site or on your book blog.

Thank you!

Ways to Support Authors

There are many ways to support
an author whose work you admire!

Request their book at your local library.

Review their book on any and all bookselling and book review sites.

Follow the author on social media and share their posts.

Take a selfie with their book and share it on social media.

Attend the author's events.

Suggest their book for your book club.

Recommend the author as a speaker or workshop leader.

Tell your friends about the book.

Include the book in a blog post or list of your favorites.

Nominate their book for an award.

Ask your local bookstore and library to stock the book.

Support the author's other projects, including pre-ordering their next book.

Add a copy of their book to your local Little Free Library.

Buy their book as a gift for someone.

Authors everywhere thank you!

ABOUT THE AUTHOR

photo credit: Lauren Volness

Angélique Jamail's poetry, short fiction, and essays have appeared in over two dozen anthologies and journals, and she's the author of *Finis.* and *The Sharp Edges of Water*. She teaches Creative Writing and English to high school students in Houston. Find her online at her blog Sappho's Torque (www.SapphosTorque.com) and on social media.

IG: angeliquejamail
Facebook: Angélique Jamail, Author
Twitter: @AngeliqueJamail